# Milly and M Morsels

"We may look different
but we feel the same."

Something was very wrong with the day.
Aunt Maude wasn't in her garden.

Stringer wasn't practising his shots.
And Mr. Burger had shut up shop.

Milly and Molly found Aunt Maude slumped
over a basket of vegetables.
"What's wrong, Aunt Maude?" they asked.

"My spinach is stunted. My potatoes are
bumpy. And my tomatoes are lopsided.
Nobody will buy them," snipped Aunt Maude.

"They'll still taste the same. Somebody will buy
them," said Milly and Molly.
"You're right. But who?" snapped Aunt Maude.

Milly and Molly found Stringer slumped over
his basketball.
"What's wrong, Stringer?" they asked.

"I've been dumped from the team," he said.
"Oh no," cried Milly and Molly. "Why."

"I don't have stamina. But don't tell me to eat my vegetables," he said. "I hate them!"

Milly and Molly found Mr. Burger slumped in his chair.

"I've been blamed for everybody's health problems," he sighed.
"But please tell me, who wants to buy a vegetable burger?"

Milly and Molly looked at one another.
"We can solve the problem... with everybody
else's problems!"

"Stringer needs to eat vegetables. Aunt Maude has just the vegetables we need to make something. And if we don't call it a vegetable something, Stringer might eat it," they said.

Mr. Burger took a moment to work that out
and then clapped his hands together.

He was out of his chair and into his apron.
Milly and Molly collected the basket of
vegetables from Aunt Maude and then rolled
up their sleeves.

Mr. Burger was back in business with an
addition to the menu … morsels.
Stringer was first in line. Milly and Molly held
their breath.

"I'll have some of those, thank you Mr.
Burger," he said. "What's in a morsel?"
"Just reds and greens," replied Mr. Burger.
Milly and Molly caught his wink.

Milly and Molly paid a grateful Aunt Maude
for her basket of vegetables and asked for
another.

Stringer was back in the team and practising his shots.

Word got about that Mr. Burger had the tastiest morsels in town.

"What's more they give you stamina," bragged Stringer.

"What's in a morsel?" asked the team.
"Just reds and greens," replied Stringer
casually.

"What are reds and greens?" asked the team,
just as Aunt Maude arrived with another
basket of vegetables.

Stringer stopped eating his morsel. He looked
at Milly and Molly.

Mr. Burger wasn't winking now.

"Reds and greens are vegetables of course,"
he said. "Milly and Molly's morsels are full of
vegetables... and stamina," said Stringer.